So You Think
You're Having a Bad Day?

So You Think
You're Having a Bad Day?

Four Stories to Make You Feel Better

Matthew Braga

iUniverse, Inc.
Bloomington

So You Think You're Having a Bad Day?
Four Stories to Make You Feel Better

iUniverse books may be ordered through booksellers or by contacting:

iUniverse
1663 Liberty Drive
Bloomington, IN 47403
www.iuniverse.com
1-800-Authors (1-800-288-4677)

ISBN: 978-1-4759-7665-6 (sc)
ISBN: 978-1-4759-7666-3 (ebk)

Library of Congress Control Number: 2013902808

Printed in the United States of America

iUniverse rev. date: 03/07/2013

Contents

Acknowledgments

I would like to thank my wife for her support in the development of these stories and my mom for the drawings.

The Best of Intentions

A couple of months ago, my wife and I were in a slump, as I suppose happens in most marriages every once in a while. We tried to work our schedules to get the same night off so we could catch up on each other's lives. My construction job would go for twelve to fourteen hours a day, so by the time I got home, she was already in bed. This went on for about a month, and then we realized we had the same Friday off.

We planned a romantic dinner for two in a nice, quiet family restaurant and hoped for a little "our time" after. We planned all of this through notes we'd been writing and leaving on the refrigerator. I had it all planned out: the flowers, the card, the wine. I even bought her favorite perfume.

Finally, Friday arrived. I had been looking forward to this for a long time. As the day progressed, I became happier and happier, to a point of almost being ecstatic. But thirty minutes before the end of the day, a main water line broke under the driveway to our construction site, along with the hopes of getting home on time. No matter how hard we worked to get things fixed, it just was not enough.

I finally got a moment to call my wife, already two hours late, and apologized. She said that she was going to get something to eat and do some thinking. *Thinking?* I thought. *That does not sound good.*

I got home about two hours after the phone call, and she was not at home. I walked into the kitchen, and on the refrigerator was a note:

Gone to Mom's for the weekend. I'll talk to you Sunday night.

My heart sank, along with the hopes of being with my wife. I took a beer from the refrigerator and sat at the dining-room table with my head in my hands. Suddenly, I thought that this would be a good time to "finish" one of my many started projects, something that we both could enjoy together. I grabbed my beer and headed for the garage. (One of the nice things about our home is that the neighbors are far enough away from us that we can make as much noise as we want without them hearing it.)

A few months before, I'd started a project that had to take a backseat: a gazebo with a hot tub. I had drawn up the plans myself and had all the wood already. I went out into the backyard with some floodlights and started digging holes for the corner poles. As I dug, I could not stop myself from smiling and feeling great anticipation for the final product.

After I got all the holes dug, I had to move all the wood out of the garage and into the backyard. I didn't think I would ever get it all out, but as I carried out the last couple of pieces, I imagined the completed project and could see people standing around, laughing and having a good time.

I shook off the daydream and started dropping posts into the holes. It was almost one in the morning when I started to mix and pour the concrete. Then I checked all the measurements one final time, shut off the lights, took a shower, and went to bed.

I got up earlier than I'd expected and headed out to a local bath-and-kitchen place, picked up the hot tub (and all that goes with it), and got back on the road. On the way home, I called a few friends, who agreed to meet me at the house to help—as long as I had the beer. One quick stop at the 7-Eleven, and I headed home with a smile and a song.

Very few things in life go the way you plan; and this was one of them. It went like clockwork. If it were an Olympic event, we would have taken the gold with no problems. The backyard was like a beehive, with the people buzzing all around. When I took my first break after six hours, I watched for a moment. It really made me feel good to see my friends come together to help me out. People were working together, laughing, and actually having a good time. No one was fighting over something trivial. No one was complaining about anything. Everyone was working together like a well-oiled machine. And most important, no one got hurt.

Twelve hours and a bunch of hot dogs, burgers, and a couple of cases of beer later, I was putting the hose in the tub to fill it. We even made a trapdoor in the floor to cover the tub when it wasn't being used. It rose to the ceiling of the gazebo and back down again on a pulley system. You could not wipe the smile off my face, even if you had a bucket of elbow grease and Comet. It was 12:30 at night when I turned on the spigot and went into the house to go to bed.

Sunday came, and I got up and cleaned the house, washed the dog, washed the car, and even cleaned the bathrooms. I was cooking dinner when I heard the key in the front door. I tried to suppress my excitement as I turned around. I heard my wife say, "You've been busy, huh?"

I noticed that she was wearing a very nice, new summer dress, had her hair done, and was looking very beautiful. "Yeah, I did a couple of things this weekend," I said with half a smile.

"Oh really? Like what?" she asked, almost in a song. She was obviously in a good mood.

"You know how you always say that I *never* finish anything?"

"Yes …" she said, with a grin starting to grow on her face.

"Have I got a surprise for *yoou*. C'mere," I said like a guy in some old movie. I had her close her eyes, and we walked hand in hand out the back door. I noticed there was water on the ground as we walked up to the gazebo.

She said, "Let me guess. You watered the backyard, right?"

"Well, kind of," I said as we stopped at the bottom of the four steps to the tub. "Okay, open your eyes," I said with a little bit of excitement in my voice.

You know that look on kids' faces at Christmas when they get exactly what they've always wanted? Times that by ten, and you will have the look on my wife's face. She didn't say anything for about five minutes. Then I turned the lights on. She just kept her mouth open and wanted to touch everything.

Finally, I said, "And that's not all." I pushed a switch, and the trapdoor in the middle started to come up, revealing the hot tub. I didn't think anyone's eyes could get so big. She was just about to say something when the pulley motor quit. The trapdoor had gotten only about six feet off the tub; it should have gone up eight feet.

She closed her mouth and said, "I am very impressed. How long before it fills up?"

I thought, *Fills up? I've had the hose in there since last night.* I said, "I'll be right back." I walked over to the spigot and saw that an animal had chewed through the hose on the back side, and half the water was coming out there and only half was in the tub. I shut it off and started back over to my wife, who was now bent over at the waist, looking into the tub.

As I walked up the stairs, I said, "Be careful. You have on your high heels—" and I missed the next step. To keep me from falling flat on my face, my hands went out in front of me. One hand hit the down switch to the trapdoor; the other landed smack dab in the middle of my wife's backside, forcing her forward. It was like Alfred Hitchcock meets National Lampoon.

I fell forward, smashing my shins on the top step and falling only halfway into the tub, ripping the buttons off my shirt. The tub was only a little less than halfway filled, and my wife had fallen into it.

Now, if that weren't enough, the trapdoor was still coming down. I could not move because my pant leg was stuck on a screwhead that didn't make it all the way in. If you really wanted to win the ten-thousand-dollar prize on *America's Funniest Home Videos*, this would have been your chance. Just as I got my pant leg unstuck, the trapdoor hit me in the middle of the back, pinning me down.

My wife, who had only twisted her ankle, later told me that she wished she had the camera when the trapdoor closed in on us. She said that as the trapdoor hit me in the back, it was like watching a scene from *The Incredible Hulk*. My face changed color, and I let out a yell that came from somewhere deep in my body. I stood straight up, still yelling, picked up the trapdoor in both hands, and held it over my head. She later told me she had been afraid that I would hurt myself, but then admitted that she was kind of impressed by the whole thing.

I held the trapdoor in both hands over my head for about a minute before I gently put it down. I looked down at her—me in my ripped pants and buttonless shirt, and her in her half-soaked dress and broken high-heeled shoe—and put my hand out to help her out of the tub. When she was standing there next to me, she tossed her wet hair over her shoulder and looked up at me with her makeup half washed off and said as straight faced as she could, "That was interesting. What else did you do while I was gone?" We laughed and limped back to the house to tend to our wounds.

I did finally fix the trapdoor problem and even finished some other projects. But every once in a while, when we are relaxing in the tub, my wife looks at me and says something like, "So, David Banner, what's your next project?"

And I respond, "Don't make me angry. You wouldn't like it when I'm angry."

Life, once again, is good.

One of *Those* Days

I've been in construction almost all of my life. My dad was in construction, his dad was in construction, and I believe even his dad was in construction. My great-great-great-grandfather came to America as a furniture maker, and I guess that's where it all started.

I was the first to join the military in my family. Being the oldest of three boys and two girls, I felt I had to set the "example." I joined the US Navy Seabees, the Navy version of the construction field. They taught me every safety program there ever was. We went through all the OSHA training, military training, and civilian safety training courses they could think of. Even though I was designated a Builder (carpenter), we were required to take all the other safety courses as well. There were the Electricians, Plumbers, Steelworkers, Mechanics, and Equipment Operators safety courses. They even threw other fields at us, like fire safety, underwater safety, aircraft safety, and even home and office safety. If it had the word *safety* in it, we got the training.

After twenty-two years of this training, I felt it was time to get out and try the civilian way of living. My wife and I bought our first home and have been living in one place now for over five years, something very different from our moving every two or three years. I have a good job, and my wife really likes the neighborhood and the neighbors.

This past summer, I built a fireplace for the living room. This is the first time we've had a working fireplace in our dwelling. We had dreams of a cozy, cool night of just the two of us sitting in front of one, curled up in each other's arms, sipping hot cocoa, and listening to soft music. Just the thought of it made us wish for winter to come early.

Well, it was the beginning of October, and I still hadn't cut any wood for the fireplace. So, one Saturday morning, I got up early with the thought of spending a couple of hours chopping wood and piling it up nice and neat to be the envy of the neighborhood. I grabbed a cup of coffee and a couple of donuts that we'd had for a week and a half and stepped out on the pouch to watch the sun rise over the backyard and my wife's prize-winning flowerbed. The donuts were stale, of course, but I thought that they were better than some Navy chow I'd had. And besides, the coffee helped wash them down.

When I finished, I walked into the bathroom and didn't realize that the window was open. With the window open, there is no pressure in the room, so when I closed the door, it slammed with a shock wave that raced through the house, waking everything and everybody. Out of nervousness, I opened the door as quietly as I could and in a soft, raspy voice said, "Sorry," and gently closed it again. Now, on most days, that would have been acceptable, but when your wife is not feeling well due to a cold that has lasted much longer than it should have, what I'd done was grounds for capital punishment.

As I stood there in my shorts, washing my face with a very lathery form of soap, my wife threw the door open and it slammed against the wall with a bang. For the first time in as far back as I could remember, I almost screamed out of fright. The only reason I didn't scream was because the air I inhaled for the scream sucked in almost all the soap I had on my face.

My wife, on a rampage, started with "Why are you up so early on a Saturday morning making so much noise? Knowing full well, I am not feeling all that—" She stopped only because I had turned toward her with a strange look on my face. "What, you got something smart to say?" she said, pointing at me.

There are so many things that could go through your mind at a moment like that, but all I could think of was, *I shouldn't have eaten those stale donuts.* Yep, soap and stale donuts don't mix. Before I could look away, up they came and splattered all over her bathrobe-covered legs.

My wife, usually a pillar of strength on any other day, would have reacted differently had she not been sick. However, she was ... well ... not herself. As if to outdo me, she retaliated by throwing up on me. The only difference was that, like I said, I was in my shorts. When it was over, I looked at her as sympathetically as I could and started to ask if she was all right. As I did so, a giant soap bubble emerged from my mouth. It was like something from the *Little Rascals.*

My lovely, ill-feeling wife, who until this point had been plotting the murder of the century, looked at me, raised her hand, and popped the bubble with her index finger with one thrust of her hand. She took the towel off the rack very calmly and wiped her face and then her hands. She took off her robe and dropped it on the floor in the pile of mess, used the towel to wipe off her legs and feet, and then dropped it on the bathrobe. She looked up at me and said in a surprisingly soft voice, "I am going back to bed now." She turned and walked away without another sound. To this day, I don't know how I managed to keep myself from laughing out loud.

It took about half an hour, and a bottle of Mr. Clean, to get the bathroom back to normal. In spite of this setback, I was still determined to cut that firewood. I got myself dressed in my favorite blue jeans—wore in, not wore out—a T-shirt with Iron Man on it, a plaid shirt, and steel-toe boots. To top it off, I donned a ball cap with a picture of a beach and chair with an umbrella that said, "Wish you were here." Now I was ready for the great outdoors.

I went to the shed, pulled out my chainsaw, ax, and eight—pound splitting hammer wedge. Then I went to my shop and got my gloves and my hearing and eye protection—remembering all my safety training. Yep, look out trees, here I come.

It amazes me how much different things are between watching someone do something and doing it myself. I walked up to a tree with no leaves that I have been eyeing for a while to cut down, checked where it would fall, put on my hearing protection, and donned my eye protection and then my gloves. I was ready. Remembering from one of my many safety courses where to make my first cut, I started the chainsaw and got to work.

After making many cuts and very carefully taking out piece after piece, I reached the center. I walked around to the back of the tree and again checked where it would fall; I was still smiling and knowing this baby was going to land right where I planned. And I started to make my back cut.

At this point, for whatever reason, some thoughts crossed my mind. Do you remember that old saying about leading a horse to water? And the one about best-laid plans and all that? I thought of a couple more that escape me at the moment. As I stood there in all my safety gear, in all my planning for the perfect fall of the tree, it started to fall. At first it went very slowly, like time suddenly stopped working. I smiled, and a thought to yell, "Timber," just like in the movies, suddenly changed to fear and screams of "No, no, *NO!*"

For some reason, Murphy was hard at work on this of all days. The place where it should fall, which I had so carefully planned, was in no need of fear. Nope, for the tree that I picked, the tree that I thought was dead, still had sap running through its veins. And for whatever reason, it twisted at the last moment and made its own path. Some kind of evil force had moved it to the right—right toward the car and the house. All my safety training, all the safety lectures I'd attended, all the training I'd received and given, completely left my being. I knew I was about to become another statistic.

I jumped to the house side of the tree, and with all my might I tried to push that falling tree away from the house and car. In the moment it took for the tree to fall, I managed to push it so hard, the veins on the side of my head bulged.

I must have done something right in a past life, because in the fraction of a second that it took for the tree to fall, I was able to give it just enough persuasion to miss the house and the car—only to land in my wife's prize-winning flower garden.

Now, as I stood there, out of breath and feeling a little proud of myself that I was able to change the mind of gravity, I thought the worst was over. But who should come out to see what all the noise was about? Yep, my loving bride of over fifteen years, who should by all rights be lying in bed recovering from a touch of the flu. She emerged from our dwelling with a look of both shock and dismay. I stood there, just short of beating my chest, and said as proud as I could, "It missed the house *and* the car, dear."

She just looked at me as a statue stares at the oncoming day, not blinking, not saying anything. Then she looked at the tree, then her prize-winning flowerbed, then the tree, and then back to me. As she stood there, with her hair in every-which direction from the pillow, a clean bathrobe and slippers, and a cup of coffee, I tried to think of something to say that would make her feel better. Unfortunately for me, what came out was "Uh, how are you feeling, honey?"

She looked right at me, her mouth dropped open, and she just stared. For just a moment, I thought she was going to say something, but all she did was stare. I probably should have just gone back to work, but I thought I should try to comfort her somehow. I took two or three steps toward her, and she closed her mouth, poured the coffee out onto the pouch, walked back into the house, and slammed the door.

After about thirty seconds, I heard the coffee cup smash against the kitchen wall and then a scream that I swear they heard on the West Coast. I took two steps toward the house, thinking there was still something I could do, but a force of some kind stopped me in my tracks, and a feeling came over me as if to say, "Better not." I stood there in my indecision, and then the scream, which seemed to have lasted ten minutes, suddenly stopped. Fear draped around me like a wet, heavy blanket, and then the door opened and my heart stopped. My wife took a step into the doorway, ran her hand through her tangled hair, and said slowly, through what seemed to be a wrench-tight smile, "I'm okay. Are you all right?"

Not knowing how to answer, I just blurted out, "Yes, thank you. Is there anything I can—"

"*Good.* I'll be in the bedroom," she said and closed the door. At that moment, I thought I had lost my hearing. There were no birds singing—anywhere—no flies around, no bees buzzing, no cars on the street, and no kids playing in the park down the street. It was very, *very* quiet. Then slowly, the noises started to come back, and that wet-blanket feeling started to lift. I entertained the thought of getting something cold to drink, but decided I could wait a little longer.

I stood there for a few minutes looking at the tree, the flowers, the car, the house, and then back to the tree, thinking of all the things that could have gone wrong. I took a deep breath, put on my glasses, my hearing protection, and my gloves once more, and picked up my chainsaw. With one more deep breath I started to cut off the branches of my prize. I cut the big branches and the trunk into eighteen-inch sections, trying to remember to "stay safe" and applying every safety measure I could think of. I tried to fix what I could in the garden, but it was obvious that I was never going to bring it back to the way it was. I opted just to leave it alone and take the heat for it later.

I carted the logs to a place I had designated "the chopping area." I cleared out a few sticks so I wouldn't trip over them, and I put one of the bigger cut logs down for my base in the center of my chopping area. Then I put another cut log on top of that to split. With all the safety precautions in place, I took the hammer wedge by the head, extended my arm, and waved a circle around me, to make sure of my "safety circle"—just like they taught me in Boy Scouts. I spread apart my legs, measured the distance with my eye from the log to my stands, got a good grip on the hammer, shifted my weight one more time, and brought the hammer wedge up over my head for the first big swing.

I brought it down with (what I thought was, anyway) the force of ten men. It hit dead center with just enough force to split all the way, the first time. Let me tell you, there is nothing more satisfying (or a bigger boost to one's ego) than to split a big log in one fell swoop. Feeling like Paul Bunyan, I put one of the halves back up on the splitting post and took my stance again, thinking safety, eyes on my target. I took my breath and swung the hammer again, and again the log split in one chop. "This ain't so tough," I said to myself in a low voice.

I had split about five or six logs into eighths, most of them splitting on the first chop, when I started to feel the workout. Now, I could have stopped and taken a break, but I looked at all those logs I still had to chop and thought I would do a couple more before my break. Still paying close attention to the safety rules, I kept going, chop after chop, log after log.

I had just put a whole cut log on the block and was in midswing when I heard, "Can I have the keys to the car?" It startled me. I turned to see my wife standing there, dressed in blue jeans, one of my plaid shirts, and a jacket.

"Huh?" I said and then wished I could take it back. You see, my wife is a fifth-grade English teacher. She usually makes kids do an essay on words like *huh, duh,* and *shut up*. She looked down at the ground and gritted her teeth.

"May I have the keys to the car, *please*? I want to go and get more flowers before the store closes."

"I'm sorry about the *huh,*" I said. "And I am really sorry about the tree falling ... well, you know. It really wasn't my fault." I put down the hammer wedge and reached for the keys.

"You know, you're right," she said as she darted her stare up from the ground. "You couldn't have picked a tree that was further away from here or even in another lot. You had to pick *this* one. But you're right, it wasn't your fault."

There are times when a man, as he gets older, knows when to let it go and not say anything else. Even as I stood there, in the back of my mind I heard the voice of reason trying to calm me down, saying, "Let it go, let it go." And a wise man would listen to that voice of reason ... but not that day.

"Well, excuse me for trying to do something good. To actually finish something I started and to clear a dead tree from the yard to make it look better. To want to plan a quiet night with his wife in front of a fireplace that he built and the logs he split. To show her how much he really loves her." I handed her the keys and picked up the hammer again.

This time I took a bigger swing than I had been taking. As I pulled the hammer from the ground and swung it up over my head, I felt I was going to send this one right into the dirt. But this time something was different. Halfway through the swing down, it was moving faster, and when the hammer hit the log, it sounded like wood on wood. And the log didn't fall in half like all the other times.

I heard my wife inhale like she was trying to suck in all the air in the neighborhood. I turned to look at her, and she was looking straight up. As if time had slowed to a crawl, I looked up and saw something black right above me. I had about two seconds before it hit me. And yes, it really hit me, right between the eyes. With all my safety training, I'd forgotten one of the most important rules: check your equipment. In my haste, I'd forgotten to check for the wedge that held the head of my hammer on; it had fallen out at some point, causing the head to slide up and off.

When I came to, I was flat on my back with my head on my wife's lap and two medical guys hovering over me. I heard someone say, "I think he's coming to!" My wife was looking down at me with a sympathetic look on her face, holding a cold compress on my head and running her fingers through my hair.

The medical guys started asking me a whole bunch of questions and took my vitals. When they thought I was ready, they helped me up and got me into the ambulance. As we were getting in, one of the guys said that I was very lucky that the blunt end of the hammerhead hit me. He added, "The other end would have caused a lot more damage."

After a couple of hours at the hospital, they let me go in the care of my loving, caring wife, who said, "Let's go home, Cy-Klutz," due to the fact that I had a bump in the center of my forehead that looked like a closed eye and because my real two eyes were almost swollen shut. As she helped me get in the car and put my seat belt on, she gently kissed my cheek and said in a very soft voice, "You didn't have to go all macho man on me. I know in my heart you love me." The drugs they gave me must have been working, because I smiled and it didn't even hurt.

I had that knot in the middle of my forehead for three full days before it finally went down and I could see straight. The next weekend, I finished chopping the wood with a new hammer wedge. And I helped my wife buy new flowers and built a greenhouse to put them in.

Whenever we need wood for that fireplace now, I go down the road with a friend of mine and his pickup truck to an old wooded lot with nothing around but trees, and we do all the cutting and chopping there. It's still hard work, but now I ask my wife to rub some of that heat stuff on my shoulders.

And like most happy endings, for Christmas that year, I got a new toy. My wife bought me a hydraulic log splitter. Dead (or dying) trees, look out.

The Cat Came Back

Old man Johnson, he had trouble of his own.

He had a yellow cat that just wouldn't leave him alone.

He tried and he tried to give the cat away.

He gave it to a man going far, far away.

But the cat came back, the very next day.

The cat came back; they thought he was a goner.

But that cat came back; he just wouldn't stay away, away, away.

This is a Harry Miller folk song from the 1940s. The other verses go on to sing about the people Mr. Johnson gave the cat to.

I can relate to Mr. Johnson's frustration. The only difference is that my problem was a black cat. No,

I am not superstitious. I'm just not a ... cat lover, shall we say.

We moved into our new house about three months ago. My trouble started just about two months after that, when I noticed a stray cat that had moved into our carport. My wife was worried because the nights were getting colder with the rapid arrival of the winter season. I kept telling her that it would be fine. After all, cats like the cold, right?

When she suggested that we catch him and bring him into the house, I knew I was going to have to think of something fast for two reasons. First, I don't like cats, and second, my dog, Duke, doesn't like cats either. Last year for a Christmas present for Duke, as a joke, I gave him a stuffed cat. It lasted less than a minute. When I reminded my wife of this, she said that we could either keep the cat in a box or we could keep the dog outside. That didn't sit too well with me, and I was sure Duke wouldn't like it either. I told her that I could catch him and take him to the shelter down the road, and some kid would get him as a Christmas gift. She agreed but asked that I do it soon, because of the cold weather.

I thought, *It's just a cat. How hard can it be? Right?* Famous last words.

I went out to the carport to scout out the area. Like most carports, ours is for everything except the car. It's a catch-all for all the "stuff that we need." Looking around at the boxes stacked from the floor almost to the ceiling, I could see that the cat had been at it for a while. He had left his markings and little "cat presents" everywhere. It didn't take long before I heard him meowing. Of course, he couldn't be where I could see him—no, no. He had to be in the furthest, hardest-to-get-to crawl space you could imagine. Still, I thought, *It's just a cat.*

I went into the house and got some of Duke's food; he barked his protest at feeding another animal "his" food. I went back to the carport and thought that when the cat smelled the food, he would simply come out of hiding, lick the food off my finger, and I would pick him up, put him in a box, drive down the road, and drop him off at the shelter. What's so hard about that? Okay, so I watched a lot of Disney movies when I was a kid.

I could tell that he could smell the food, because I heard him running around the boxes. I figured it must have been a while since he'd eaten. Suddenly, he stopped moving around. It was quiet for about fifteen seconds, and then a little black cat with one white spot on his front right paw, not much older than a kitten, walked out from the corner of the room. I must admit, it was cute, but I had a job to do.

The closer he came to me, the slower he went. I knelt slowly and put my finger out to him with the food on it. He slowly moved closer and finally got close enough to the food, never for a moment taking his eyes off me. As he started to lick the food, I reached with the other hand and almost got ahold of his little neck. But I must have moved too fast, because he wanted more than just the food. With both little paws, he reached up, claws the size of sixteen-penny nails, fully extended, and grabbed ahold of both sides of my index finger.

Now, I have hit my thumb with a hammer, run a staple into my arm, caught a fishing hook in my back, and shot a nail from a nail gun into my foot (long story, another time), but that little guy inflicted enough pain in my finger that I yelled so loud the guy five houses away came out of his house to see what had happened. I stood straight up and whipped my hand back and forth with this little guy still attached. As I think about it now, the sound coming from him was like one of those toy cow sticks being shaken back and forth really fast. He hung on for what seemed like hours, but was probably only seconds, and then let go. He flew into a bunch of boxes in the corner that he had come out of.

As I gathered my composure, I ran to the corner where the cat had fled, throwing boxes out of my way. One of the boxes hit the floor, and whatever was inside smashed upon the impact. Now I had another problem. I walked slowly over to the box. In big print on its side was written, "Mom's Dishes—Fragile." Talk about letting the wind out of your sails. I forgot about the cat long enough to pick up the box and hide it under some other boxes against the wall.

As I stood there looking for the cat, my hand began to throb. That's when I noticed I was bleeding. I went into the house, washed my hands, and put a bandage on my wounds. Now I really had to catch this cat.

As I was walking out of the house, my wife called from the family room: "How's it going?" Of course

I said with a song in my voice, "I almost have him. This won't take long." I headed back out of the house heading toward the carport.

Now I was like a lion on the hunt. I *was* going to catch this little terror. I grabbed an empty box and put in some of Duke's food, to which he growled his second protest at me. I laid the box on its side with the top open. I duct-taped the two sides and one flap down so that when the cat was inside, all I would have to do is close the one side. Sounded easy enough. I waited in a chair not far from the box, behind a piece of wood-grain paneling that I was saving for ... someday. I didn't move.

And I didn't have to wait long before that little ... cat came out and slowly walked over to my little trap. As he got closer, I could feel the anticipation build inside of me. *He's almost there,* I thought, giving one of those Grinch grins. The cat, at the edge of the box, looked around one more time before he gave in to temptation and entered the box. I waited just long enough to make sure he had started eating, and then I pounced on the box and closed it with lightning speed that would impress a cat of any size. I had him.

I duct-taped the top closed, leaving a space between the two halves of the top flaps for air, and I tossed the box onto the front seat of my car. I went into the house and told my wife I had to run to the store and asked if she needed anything.

"Maybe some milk and bread," she said. "Oh, how about something for supper?"

"I'll be right back," I said with that little song in my voice.

I got into the car and looked at the box with my prisoner in it. His little paw was jetting in and out of the opening. I grabbed a pen and teased him for about a minute with it. Then I started the car and headed for the pound.

It was a nice Saturday afternoon, and as I drove through the neighborhood, I could see people putting up their Christmas decorations. With a little nip in the air, it was starting to feel like Christmas. I turned on the radio and sang along with some of the carols. Before I knew it, I had driven the three miles to the pound. "And what to my wondering eyes did appear?" I sang as I pulled up to the pound. A sign on the front gate read, "Closed until Wednesday. Sorry for the inconvenience."

"*Sorry for the inconvenience?!* You have no idea!" I said at the sign, which did not answer me. I looked at the box, with the little paw jetting in and out, and then I looked at the sign, then the box, then at the sign. I finally said, "No way."

I put the car in reverse, backed out into the street, peeled out, and headed for the store, only a block away. When I got there, I parked at the end of an almost empty lot, with the passenger's door away from the store. I got out and walked around the car and opened the door, pulled out the box, and looked around quickly for witnesses. Not seeing anyone, I opened the box and shook out my little friend. He hit the road running. I watched him run across the parking lot and into a field, where some kids were playing. I thought for sure he would find someone there to take him home. Happy with myself, I put the box back in the car, closed the door, and went into the store to pick up some stuff.

I like going to the store on two occasions. First is when there are not a lot of people around and the lines are short or nonexistent. Second is when I know exactly what I want and know right where to find it. In and out. I think I set a new record today. In and out in less than four minutes. I thought maybe I'd call Ripley's.

I got back to the car, looked around one more time, got in, and drove home. I was still singing Christmas carols when I stopped the car in the driveway and got out, grabbed the bags, and closed the door. As I walked to the house, I got a strange feeling I was being watched. There he was, sitting on a box in the carport, the black cat with a white spot on his front right paw. I stood there frozen like someone had shot me with a ray gun. For a split second, I thought I was dreaming, but when he meowed, I dropped the bag with the jar of tomato sauce, and it smashed on the sidewalk. This, of course, sent the cat running for the boxes.

The front door popped open, and my wife ran out. "Are you all right? I thought I heard something break."

"Yeah, I'm fine. I tripped over ..." I looked around to see what I could blame it on and said, "the lip in the driveway."

At first she didn't say anything, and I didn't think she bought it. But then she said, "I told you not to drag your feet, but you don't listen to me, no, no ..." Her voice trailed off as she went back into the house. I just bit my lip and glared back into the carport, looking from side to side.

I took the rest of the stuff from the store into the house and put it on the counter in the kitchen. Then I went back outside to clean the tomato sauce off the sidewalk. This time when I went for Duke's food, he actually stood in front of the shelf we keep the cans of Alpo in, defying me to take any more. Sometimes I think he thinks he's human. As he stood there looking up at me, I did what anyone else would have done: I knelt down and reasoned with him.

"Look, boy, if I don't get rid of this cat, he will take over. I know you don't want that, do you? Having to share your toys, your bed ..." I looked over at his bowl. "And maybe even your food." Then I looked back at him and said, "Do you really want that to happen?"

Just then my wife came into the room. "Who are you taking to?" Duke looked at her and back at me, let out what sounded like a sigh, and walked out of the room with his head hung down, as if to say, "Do what you want."

"Scary, simply scary," I said as we watched him go and lie down in his bed with his back toward us.

"What's going on here, anyway?" my wife finally said.

"Nothing," I said with a half-smile. "Just having a little talk with Duke, that's all."

Looking at me kind of sideways, she asked, "So how's the Big Cat hunting going?"

"It's going just fine," I said as I stood up. "In fact, that's just what I was talking to Duke about when you came in. I was telling him how important it is that I use some of his food to catch this 'Big Cat,' and he agreed. He is a very smart dog, you know."

"Riiggghhhhtttt." She turned and walked out the door.

Back to the hunt.

Since it had worked so well the first time, I opened the box with duct tape on it, laid it down on its side again, put some more dog food in it, and hid behind my piece of paneling. This time I waited about fifteen minutes before the cat came out from his hiding place. He was still acting very cautious; I could see him from a very small nail hole I had made in the panel. He looked around and slowly walked up to the box, sniffed the air, looked around one more time, and slowly entered the box.

I waited—then I grabbed the box and closed the lid. I reused the duct tape and put the box in the car. I went into the house and told my wife that I was going to get some more tomato sauce for supper and that I would be right back. I got in the car, and again that little paw with the white spot on it was jetting in and out of the lid. I thumped the lid with my middle finger one time, and the paw disappeared into the darkness of the box.

This time, knowing that the pound was closed, I drove six miles down the road to the next town. The cat kept meowing, so I turned up the radio to drown out the noise. I drove into a school parking lot, which was empty, and parked in the back near the woods. I thought for sure he would never find his way back this time.

I got out of the driver's door, and as I walked around the car to the passenger's side, I looked around to see if there were any people. The coast was clear. I opened the door, grabbed the box, and took about six steps from the car. I shook the box twice and yelled at it, "Don't come back this time." I opened one side of the lid away from me and laid the box down on its side.

That's when I saw the hole in the bottom of the box. I turned back to the car and then back to the box. I picked it up and looked inside. Yep, empty. I ran back over to the car and looked inside. Nothing. From an angle, I looked under the seats, not wanting to get all the way down, for fear of having the cat run out from under the seat and scratch my face to pieces. *It must have run out when I was walking away from the car with the box,* I thought. *Yeah, that's what happened.* I turned around and looked to see if I could see it. Then I closed the door and walked back over to the driver's door, still looking around. Just before I got in the car, I saw something in the ball field, something small. "That's it," I thought out loud, and I got in the car and started to the store.

I did mention that I watched a lot of Disney when I was growing up, but I also watched all the Steven King movies as well. Anyone who has seen *Pet Cemetery* knows what I'm talking about. Out of panic, I kept looking around the car for this cat from hell, and what made it really scary was I didn't see it. The mind can do some funny things, given the right circumstances.

After a couple of miles, I turned on the radio to try to relax to another Christmas carol. I started to hum along. I was only about half a mile away from the store when I heard a scratching noise coming from the back speaker. I turned and saw ... a black cat with giant claws shredding my backseat.

Now, the next five seconds seemed to take five minutes. I spun around to grab the cat, which he obviously knew I was going to do. So, as I reached, he jumped. I pulled the steering wheel right and tried to grab the cat in midair as we drove off the road and over a mailbox with a chicken statue on the top. I turned around to face front and cut the wheel all the way to the left as we drove into a gutter filled with wet, cold muck and grass. The car bottomed out and bounced up as I gained a little traction. I was heading back onto the street and right for a garbage truck. Reacting as quickly as I could, I cut the wheel as hard as I could back to the right and jammed the brakes. This was bad for two reasons. One, it put the car into a little spin. Two, and more painful, the cat had jumped up and out of my reach and was on the headrest of the seat behind me. When I jammed the brakes, it catapulted him to the back of my head. I had thought that my finger hurt badly when he grabbed it for the food. Heh. That cat flew through the air with all *four* paws, claws extended in front of it like some kind of, I don't know, cat missile in some cartoon.

So, with all four paws and claws stuck to my head, in a car swerving out of control, Christmas music blaring, "Tis the season to be jolly," the garbage truck driver blaring his air horn, and me screaming like a little girl, I floored the gas pedal to get out of the way of the truck. We slid back into the gutter and over the neighbor's mailbox with the John Deere tractor on it, completely missing the garbage truck by a fraction of an inch, and sliding to a halt in a driveway.

When my car came to a complete stop, I swung the door open and jumped out like the car was full of bees. The driver of the garbage truck was almost all the way over to my car already, and the man that used to own the John Deere tractor mailbox was coming out of his house. They both saw the headgear I was sporting and heard me screaming, "Get it off! *Get it off!*" The driver got to me first and went to grab the cat; it turned and hissed at him as if to say, "He's mine. Get back!" This made the driver take a few steps back.

The other man, the one from the house, must have been in his eighties, and no cat was going to scare him. He reached up and thumped the cat on the head. I have never heard such a thump in all my life. The cat went unconscious for about two seconds. This relaxed it long enough for it to let go of my head, which was *really* hurting by now. The man grabbed it by the scruff of its neck and started to walk away with it. Then he stopped, turned around, and asked with a half-smile, "Do you still want him?"

"*No way!*" I yelled, but then calmed down a little and said, "Umm, no thank you. If you want him, you're welcome to the little ... I mean, you can have him."

The man turned around and let the cat down in the grass. It took off for the barn. From what I could see, the man had about a ten—or fifteen-acre farm. He said, "I could always use another cat to keep the mice out of my barn. Are you okay, sonny?"

With my head pounding, I answered, "Yes, sir. I am really sorry about your mailbox. I'll buy you a new one."

"No need for that, young fella. About a year ago, I had some trouble with the local teenagers driving past and smashing the mailboxes with their baseball bats. I bought a few extra mailboxes. I'm not going to let them think they got the best of me. No, sir."

Still rubbing my head, I said, "I should go over and apologize to your neighbor."

"No need to bother yourself with that either. I've been taking care of Patti since her husband died last July. I have a supply of mailboxes for her too." He paused and said, "You really should get your head looked at."

The garbage truck driver and I looked at each other and then at the old man. He added, "I mean, go get some first aid for your wounds. The cat will be fine. You can come back and visit with him whenever you want to."

"That's okay. I ..." I stopped to think for a moment and finished a little slower. "I can see he will be just fine here, chasing mice and all." I shook his hand and added, "Thank you very much. Merry Christmas." Then I turned to the truck driver and said, "Do I owe you anything?"

"Nope. But that was some mighty fine maneuvering there, worthy of any stunt car driving on any Saturday afternoon TV if I ever saw one. But, umm, maybe you should leave it to them from now on, okay?"

I stuck out my hand and said, "You can count on it." He shook my hand a little too vigorously, and my head bounced a little. I had to grab it with both hands to keep it from what felt like falling off. He apologized, turned, and walked away.

I got into my car, turned off the radio, which was still blaring Christmas music, backed up, and drove home as it started to get dark. I pulled into the driveway just as the streetlights came on and parked like I always do. I sat there in the car for a few more minutes, taking in the strange afternoon, then got out, and—in a unconscious movement—looked into the carport, half-scared and half-angry. Nothing moved. No animals in sight. I drew a deep breath, and to try to hide some of the blood, I pulled my hat down as far as I could without hurting myself more.

I opened the front door. My wife, who was sitting there in the family room, turned with a sigh of relief and said, "Where have you been? I was getting worried."

"I, umm, ran into an old friend and started to talk and ..." Just then something caught my eye in the corner where Duke's bed was. "I, umm, we were, umm ... What's that?" I asked, squinting to try to see better as I pointed at Duke's bed. Duke was lying there, but something dark was lying next to him. Something dark ... with a white spot on its front paw.

"*No way! No way possible*," I shouted like a crazy person.

"Honey, calm down. It's just the cat that was living in the carport. I didn't want to tell you this, because I know how much you don't like cats," she said in a voice that could tame the wildest of beasts.

"No, dear, you don't understand. That cat is evil. It is possessed or something, sent to us right from hell. We have to get out of here before it's too late! *Please!*" I grabbed her hand and was dragging her toward the front door. "We don't have much time. Come on!"

"Stop it. Stop it right now!" she said as she ripped her hand out of mine. "You are not making any sense. I've been feeding this cat and his brothers now for a little more than a week. They are fine."

Grabbing her hand again, not wanting to look away from the dark corner of the room, I whispered, "I'll explain after we get to a safe place. After I know we are safe frommm ... " It was like a slap in the face. I looked at her and I let go of her hand. "His brothers?"

"Yes," she said, looking at me kind of sideways, not knowing if she should give me a chance to explain or call a psychologist. "I've been feeding them. It's the strangest thing, though. All three are black with a ... "

"White spot on their front right paw," I said slowly in a low voice.

"Yes, that's it. So you have seen them. Do you know were the other two are?"

I looked over at Duke, who was still lying down with his head up and his new best friend next to him. I whispered, "Traitor." And just as if he understood me, he put his head down between his front paws and let out a sigh.

I turned and started toward the bedroom, and my wife said, "Well, are you going to tell me what happened or not?"

"Or not," I said over my shoulder and kept walking.

After a hot shower and something to eat, I told my wife about the day I'd had. She sat quietly, and when I was finished, I asked, "Well, what do you think?"

After a long moment, she said, "I think three things. First, you will replace my mother's dishes. Second, you forgive Duke; it's really not his fault. And third, you give the cat a chance. I don't think we are going to find the cat in the field, and the second one sounds like it might be with someone who will take care of him." Then she paused, and in a soft voice asked, "How's your head?"

"It finally stopped pounding, thanks to you cleaning out the cuts." After a long pause, I added, "I'll give the cat a chance, but I'm not promising anything." Just then the cat jumped up on my lap and purred. My wife smiled.

It's been a couple of weeks now. Duke and Lucky, as we have come to call him, get along great, eat from the same bowl, sleep in the same bed. Stranger than fiction. And me, well, today I finished closing up the carport and putting a screen door in the front. I told my wife I was winterizing it, but I think she thinks I'm animal proofing it. She's right.

Adventures with a Worry War~~d~~*t*

Once there was a little boy named Ward. His father called him that because Warden, the boy's full name and the name of the great-grandfather he was named after, was used only when he was in trouble. All his friends called him Wart, because he worried about everything. Every morning, Ward would wake up and say, "What's going to happen to me today?"

"Come down for breakfast, Ward. And bring your little sister," his mom would call.

"Not again!" he would call back.

"If I'm going to be the babysitter, can I get paid?"

"Warden! Do as your mother says," his dad would reply.

"Okay, okay. I'm coming."

His sister, Mary, would be standing in her crib with her arms reaching out whenever Ward walked into the room. "I'm coming, Little Bit." That was his nickname for her, because when she was born, he said, "Why is she only a little bit big, Mom?"

As he was trying to open the crib, he pinched his finger in the latch that opened the gate. "Ouch!" he yelped. All his sister could do was giggle and put her arms up again as if to say, "Let me out!"

"So you thought that was funny, huh?" Ward said. "I'll show you something funny." He began to tickle her under the arms. She started to laugh and kick her feet. The harder she laughed, the harder she kicked. And then *wham*, she kicked her brother right in the chin. "Ouch!" he yelled again. All his sister could do was smile.

As he rubbed his chin, he said, "That's enough. Time for breakfast. I hope nothing happens on the way downstairs." He had spoken too soon. As he helped his sister down out of the crib, he saw one of his toys under the desk. "There it is," he said. "I've been looking for that thing for a week now." As he ducked his head and went under the desk, Little Bit came up behind him and lost her balance. On her way down, she reached out and grabbed the first thing she saw, her brother's pants. He raised his head and slammed it into the desk.

"What's going on up there?" his dad said.

"Nothing," Ward said as he crawled out from under the desk, rubbing his head. He looked at his sister, and all she could say was, "Oops, Soaree, Wart."

"Stop calling me that," he said. "Let's get to breakfast before mom gets really upset."

They got downstairs without anything else going wrong. As Ward got settled at the table, his dad said, "Are you ready for the big baseball game on Saturday?"

"I don't think I'm going to play."

"What?!" his mother exclaimed. "You've been talking about this game for weeks."

"I know, Ward said sadly. "But what if it rains? What if they don't let me play? What if I get hurt? I don't want to get hurt, do I?"

"Well, no," his dad said in a low voice. "But you can't go through life worrying about what's going to happen from one day to the next."

"And what about your friends?" his mom asked. "Won't they be upset? After all, you did say that you would play, didn't you?"

"Well, yeah, only because you told me to."

"I beg your pardon?" his dad said in a voice that was a little louder than normal. "You asked us what we thought about you playing on this Little League team, and we told you that we thought it would be good for you. We never told you that you *had* to play. The final decision was yours. We told you that we would back you up in whatever you wanted to do. I don't remember telling you that you had to do this or else."

Ward just sat there staring at his cereal. He knew his dad was right. Secretly he wanted to play ball with all his friends, but he thought they would all laugh at him.

"Nobody likes a quitter," his dad said. "But, if you really don't want to play, we won't make you. Right, Mom?"

"That's right," she said lightheartedly. "You're going to be ten years old next month. I think it's time for you to make your own decision about what you want to do in your free time."

"So if I don't want to go to school—" Ward started to say, but his dad said sternly, "Your mother said *free* time." There was a moment of silence and then, almost on cue, they all started laughing.

At school, things were pretty normal. And by *normal*, I mean the things that happened to Ward happened every day. He got to his locker, and like every other morning, it took five tries to open it.

"Trouble with your lock again, *Wart?*" came that voice. A voice that sent chills down the spine of every kid in school. It was Wayne, the school bully. He was bigger than the rest of the kids, and he used that to his advantage. His IQ and his shoe size were about the same number, but he knew how to get the other kids' attention.

"Whatcha bring in for me today, *Wart?*" Every day, all the kids had to bring in something for protection pay for Wayne. It really was protection *from* him, but no one ever said that out loud. "Well, whatcha got?"

Ward just stood there. Other kids stopped and gathered around, like they did every other morning. They all gave up their things: lunch, money, drinks, even homemade cookies that their moms made special for them. They gave it up to avoid a gathering like the one that Ward brought on every morning.

Lately, Ward had been taking longer and longer to pay up. He really was tired of it. After all, he was going to be ten years old next month, and he worried about making it till then. But this was really bothering him.

"You know ... " Ward started to say and then trailed off.

"You know *what,* Wartmeister? Are you worried what's going to happen to you if you don't pay me? You should. You really should. And I'll do it too, right here in front of everyone. And you know what? They won't see a thing, because they know what will happen if they tell. Don't you?" he yelled at everyone. No one said a word. They didn't like the fact that he was threatening them all the time, but what could they do? He was so much bigger than them. He would surely put a hurting on them.

"What's it going to be, bud?"

"Okay, okay," Ward said as he took out the money his dad had given him for lunch and gave it to Wayne. "Someday, Wayne, you'll—" Wayne stepped into him, thrusting his chest into Ward's face.

"Someday I'll *what*, pinhead? You are going to do something? Oooo, I am so scared! Please don't hurt me, Mr. Wart!" he said sarcastically. Then his whole attitude changed back to the tough guy. "Don't make me laugh, twerp. I'd smash you without even breaking a sweat." Then Wayne pushed him up against the lockers and said, "I'm glad you had your payment. I wouldn't want anything to happen to you, Wart. Remember that, will ya?"

With that, Wayne pushed his way through the crowd of kids that had stopped to see who the next victim of the Night Crawler would be. One of Ward's friends had thought up that nickname because, so the story goes, when Wayne was a baby, he would get out of his crib at night when his parent were asleep. He would go outside to play in the sandbox and somehow make it back to his bed before they woke up the next morning, only to find him covered in dirt. Ward and his friends believed that he still did it, but they never talked about it out loud for the fear that someone might hear them and use it later to get themselves out of trouble with Wayne. Now that the show was over, the crowd started to disperse, and only Ward's friends stuck around to try to support him.

"I really wish someone would do something about him," said Mike, Ward's oldest and closest friend.

"And who, pray tell, is going to do it? You?" Janet asked. She was pessimistic on any subject. You would say that the sky was blue, and she would say that it was aqua. Say the grass is dark green and she would say, "No, it's forest green." But everyone let her stick around because she had a great imagination. She was reading something all the time. She really liked mystery novels. She was always imagining that she was at a crime scene, looking for clues.

"Don't let him get to you, Ward," Amanda said. "He will get what's coming to him. He'll get his." Ahh, Amanda, the best-looking girl in school. And she was smart too. Very smart—a straight-A student. She liked hanging around with Ward and his friends because they treated her like anyone else. Her parents were always asking her to find friends closer to her "intelligence level," whatever that meant. But they were all equal in the group, each of them with his or her own special gift. Ward liked to see how things worked, so he was always taking things apart and putting them back together. Mike liked to design things. Janet had her imagination, and Amanda had confidence that inspired them all. When the four of them got together, they could do anything.

"I won't let him get to me today, or any other day," Ward said. "But you're right. He will get what's coming to him." He watched the Night Crawler walk away. "He will get his."

Then came the part of the day that Ward dreaded the most: gym class. So many things could go wrong there. He'd take his time getting into his shorts and T-shirt. Then he'd walk as slowly as he could to the gym floor.

"Ward! Get out here, now!" Mr. Jenkins yelled. "Every day it's the same thing with you. I think you owe the class an apology." His voice always seemed louder when it echoed off the big walls of the gym.

"I'm sorry for making you wait. But some day you'll thank me—"

"That's enough, Ward," Mr. Jenkins said in a low voice.

"'Cause you'll be rushing out here and you're gonna slip and fall and hurt yourself, and who will be to blame—"

"That's enough, Ward!" Mr. Jenkins's voice was a little louder.

"The school, that's who. And will they do anything about it?"

"Ward, if you finish that sentence, you're going to the Big Room." That's the term all the teachers used for the principal's office, because it was, it seemed, almost as big as the gym. Ward got in line for attendance.

When he was finished, Mr. Jenkins said, "Since we have the Little League game tomorrow, we will spend today practicing, to give you the chance to play like it is the real game." Some booed and some cheered. "That's enough. We are going outside now, and that's the end of it. Let's go!"

All Ward could think was, *Outside?* Was this gym teacher insane? Surely he knew what could happen to you if you went out on a day like this. If it was cloudy, it could rain, and they all would get sick for sure. If it wasn't cloudy, they could all get sunburned. And what about the bugs? The scientists on the Discovery Channel said that the flying insects of today carry all kinds of diseases and stuff that can make you sick. And then there's pollen. They were surely walking into a trap, a trap that they could not escape.

It was a beautiful day. The sun was shining, the birds were singing, and there was a light breeze blowing. It was perfect baseball weather. So what was Ward so worried about? I guess nothing. They got out to the ball field, and they chose teams, and just like Ward thought, he was picked last. They even picked Judy before him, and she was the clumsiest girl in the whole school.

Everyone got a chance at bat, and everyone got a chance in the field. Mr. Jenkins was yelling out instruction to everyone as the game went on.

"Swing when the ball is closer to you, Sue."

"You have to go toward the ball, not run away from it when it's hit, Darrin."

For thirty grueling minutes, the two teams got a chance to hit and play the field.

"Last ups," Mr. Jenkins yelled as Ward's team got to bat. Ward was fifth in line. He was saying under his breath, "Great! For the first time things are going my way. I won't have to bat, because the people in front of me will definitely strike out before I have to get up there." Brian grabbed a bat and went to home plate.

"Strike one, strike two, strike three, you're out."

"Yes!" said Ward.

"Joel, you're up," Mr. Jenkins yelled.

"Strike one, strike two, strike three, you're out."

"This is great," Ward said with growing confidence. He started to smile from ear to ear.

"Judy, you're up." Ward could hardly hold back his enthusiasm.

"Strike one, strike two ... ball one, ball two, ball three." Ward shifted uneasily where he was standing. "Ball four. Take a base." Judy was so happy, she screamed with excitement and giggled all the way to first base.

"That's okay, that's okay," Ward kept saying.

"Tony, you're up."

"Come on, Tony. You can strike out. You can do it," Ward said under his breath. On his first swing, Tony connected. Ward's stomach dropped. "Foul ball," yelled Mr. Jenkins.

"Shooo, I thought it was in there," Ward said out loud.

"What was that, Ward?" Mr. Jenkins asked.

Ward was petrified. "Think quick, think quick," he said to himself. "Umm, all I said was, 'Man, I thought that was in there,' Mr. Jenkins."

Mr. Jenkins looked sideways at him and yelled to the pitcher, "Let's play."

Ward looked nervously around him as the pitcher threw the ball. Everything slowed down. As the ball got closer to Tony, his facial expression went from scared to confident in a matter of seconds. Tony swung with all his might and connected with it at just the right speed. The ball went sailing out to center field, where the player was watching a bird fly overhead. The ball landed only about a foot away from where the fielder was standing. Julie, who was playing center field, screamed out of fright. Tony screamed out of joy and ran all the way to first base.

Mr. Jenkins was about to call Ward to bat when he looked at his watch. Ward just knew he was going to be called and was going to embarrass himself in front of the whole class. "Saved by clock," called Mr. Jenkins. He looked at Ward and yelled, "Let's go in." Ward was so happy he skipped all the way back to the locker room.

The rest of the afternoon was uneventful, which just meant that there was nothing to worry about.

That night at the supper table, Ward's dad asked how his day went. At first, Ward was quiet, just moving his carrots from one side of the plate to the other. Then he slowly started to tell his mom and dad about his math class, then social studies, then health. He sat quietly again for a moment. Then, as fast as he could, he blurted out, "We went outside for baseball. May I be excused?" He jumped up out of the chair and started for the door.

"Not so fast there, young man," his dad said in that low voice he used when he wanted undivided attention. It stopped Ward right in his tracks. "What are you not telling us?"

Ward felt like he was standing there for hours before he finally turned around. He cleared his throat and said something in a very low voice.

"Your voice is like a car," his dad said. "The more gas you give it, the louder it gets. So step on the gas and try again."

Ward stood up straight, put his shoulders back, and in a clear voice said, "I am just worried about tomorrow's game, that's all." Then, like a balloon deflating, he slouched again.

His dad said in a calm voice, "Okay. Come back here and sit down, and let's talk about it." Ward walked over to the table and sat down in the chair he'd just gotten up from.

His dad said again in a calm voice, "My dad used to say that negative thoughts breed negative results. Do you understand what that means?"

Ward, wanting the conversation to be over, looked up at him, shifted in his chair, and nodded.

His dad looked down at the table, closed his eyes, and said, "I can tell by the blank look on you face, you do not." Ward just smiled.

His dad opened his eyes again and looked up at Ward. "If you believe you can't do something, you won't be able to do something. If you really believe you cannot play baseball, then you will never be any good at it. You have to think positively if you want to get anywhere in life. How do you think George Washington felt that night crossing the Delaware? Or how Abraham Lincoln felt before he ordered the Civil War? They really had to *believe* in what they were about to do, or they would have never accomplished what they needed to do. We are all called on to do something with our life. Sometimes it's something small, and sometimes it's something really big. Sometimes we get to choose what it is, and sometimes it is forced upon us. No matter what it is, we all need to do our best, whether it's for ourselves or for our country."

Ward sat there for a few minutes just thinking, looking at his feet as they swung back and forth. Though he still was nervous about the ball game, he did feel better about it.

His dad said, "Are you okay? Do you understand now? Do you have any questions?"

"I do understand more now. You've given me a lot to think about. It might help me to think if I had some dessert, though," he said, half-looking up at his dad.

His dad gave a quick laugh and said, "I was just thinking the same thing." He looked at his wife and asked, "May we have two desserts, please?"

Little Bit chimed in with "Free!" as she held up three fingers.

After dessert, Ward helped clear the table, played for fifteen minutes with his LEGOs, and then helped Little Bit get ready for bed. He was brushing his teeth and still thinking of what his dad had said: negative thoughts breed negative results. He got into bed thinking of the day's events and of what his dad had said, about school, about the events with the Night Crawler, *and* about the ball game. The last thing he noticed before he fell asleep was his calendar on the wall with a picture of the Three Stooges painting a house. Larry was walking under the ladder, and Curly was on the ladder, spilling the paint on him, and Moe was yelling at both of them. Ward turned out the light and thought it would take a long time to fall asleep. His head was spinning: negative thoughts, math class, Night Crawler, ball game, ladders, gym class, Three Stooges, negative thoughts … negative thoughts … negative …

"Hey, Wart! It's time to go to the game, nuck, nuck, nuck." Ward opened his eyes and saw Curly standing next to his bed in painter's clothes and in black and white, but the rest of the room was in color.

"Leave him alone, numbskull." Ward turned to the other side of the bed and saw Moe, who looked the same way—in black and white and in painter's clothes. And his hat was on sideways. "Can't you see he's worried enough without you making all that noise?"

"Come on, it's time for breakfast," he heard Larry call from the door. Both Moe and Curly ran to the door, bumping into each other—with Moe winning out, of course.

Ward shook his head and asked out loud, "Did that really happen?" He got up and noticed he was dressed for the game already. He walked downstairs and saw Moe, Larry, and Curly sitting at the table eating breakfast and making jokes. When Curly knocked over the salt on the table, Moe went to smack him, saying, "Why I oughta. Now look what you've done. Clean it up!"

Ward walked into the kitchen and saw Mr. Jenkins making breakfast. "How many pancakes do you want, sport? You better eat a lot, because you *will* bat today, I assure you."

Then Tony walked into the kitchen and said, "May I have more pancakes, Mr. Jenkins? Oh, morning, Worry Wart. Did you see me make it to first base? Will you make it today?"

"Of course he will." Ward turned around and saw Judy standing there, in his house. She had *never* been to his house.

Ward walked out the back door and started down the sidewalk to the ball field. Though the sun was shining where he was, it was cloudy over the ball field. He looked down at the sidewalk and noticed it was full of cracks. "Step on a crack, you break your mama's back, nuck, nuck, nuck," Curly said behind him. "It's *mother's*, half-wit, not *mama's,*" Moe said as he slapped Curly across the face. "Guys, *guys!* Look!" Larry said with excitement.

There was a line of people about two blocks long, single file, to get into the ball field, and they were all walking under a ladder to get in. "That can't be good," Ward said. As he got closer, he noticed that the guys at the gate were handing out something. When Ward was only a few people away, he could see that they were handing out wooden bats, and the line was all the way to home plate, where everyone was taking a turn at bat.

When he got to the gate, they handed him a metal bat, and that was when he noticed the thunder and lightning. When he got to the edge of the field, his dad came over and stopped him by putting his arm up in front of his bat. His dad looked down and said, "We are here for you, Ward, your mom and me. We always have been and always will be."

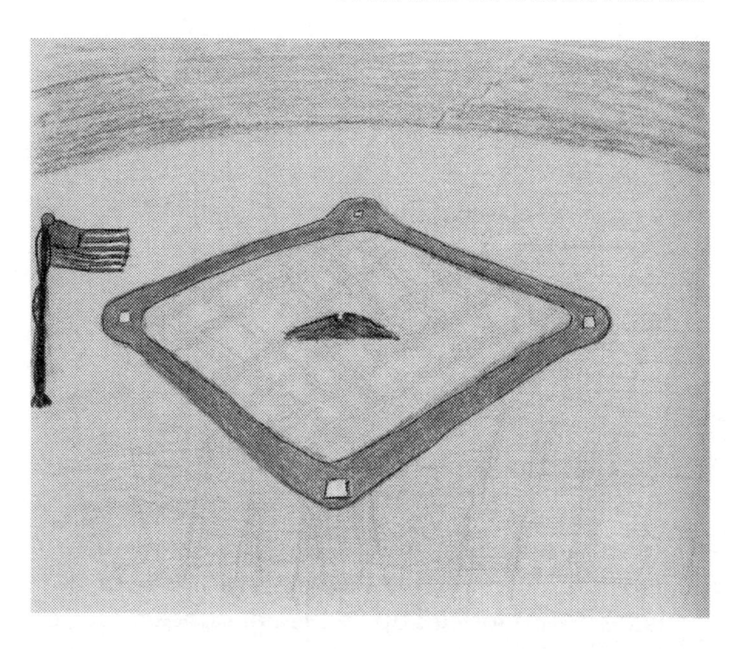

When the person in front of him batted, the whole stadium began to chant, "Ward, Ward, he's our man. If he can't do it, no one can." The crowd got louder and louder until it was deafening. When it got very loud, his dad lowered his arm and waved Ward to home plate. The crowd went wild with cheering. As he walked up to the plate, a black cat walked across his path. Ward could have sworn he saw the black cat mouth his name in unison with the crowd. He got to home plate and looked at the pitcher. It was Moe. Then he heard behind him, "Hey, kid, hit a homey, nuck, nuck, nuck." Ward turned to see Curly as the catcher and then noticed Larry was covering first base—all three still in black and white.

"Play ball," he heard the umpire yell, and then he noticed the umpire was his math teacher, Mr. Lees, with his long hair in a ponytail, his thick-rim glasses, and his red bowtie. And playing shortstop was none other than the Night Crawler. Ward's dad was umpiring first base, and his mom was umpiring third base. He had to squint to see who was near second base, but when he recognized her, he broke out in the biggest smile he could have ever had. Amanda—with her flowing blonde hair, eyes of blue, and skin of fine porcelain, like she had just walked out of a movie set.

"And next up to bat is our own local hero, *Ward Jenkins*!" The crowd went wild with cheers and whistles. Ward looked up to the announcer's booth and saw that Mike and Janet were the announcers. It seemed all his family and friends where there. And, boy, was he nervous.

The crowd quieted down, the thunder rolled across the sky, and the first pitch was ... bowled? It rolled across the ground, bouncing up every couple of feet, and slowed down just before it rolled over home plate and stopped just on the other side of it.

"*Strike one!*" yelled the umpire. The crowd started yelling and booing.

Ward turned around and yelled, "*What?!*"

Mr. Lees lifted up his face mask and said, "You should have turned in your homework on time yesterday, huh?" Ward just shook his head, and then looked back at the pitcher. The crowd settled down.

Moe looked to Curly for the signal. A fly was buzzing around Curly's face, so he was swatting at it, but Moe thought it was the signal and threw the ball straight up in the air. It sounded like the whole crowd inhaled at the same time. The ball went up, up, up for what seemed like five minutes, and then came down with a bolt of lightning behind it. It landed in front of home plate with a loud crack of thunder, which made Ward jump back. "*Strike two!*"

"You have to be kidding, right?" Ward yelled. Again, boos erupted from the crowd.

Mr. Lees looked at the crowd and then put his hands up to quiet them, saying, "Okay, okay. Ball one." The crowd burst out in cheers.

The pitcher wound up and threw a very slow ball, which took about ten minutes to get to home plate. Ward knew this was it. He waited as the tension got stronger and stronger. Then, just when he thought he would burst, he swung the bat as hard as he could. Flashes from every camera in the crowd were flashing as he heard the cheers like they were coming from a tunnel. Just as the ball was above the plate, his bat suddenly weighed fifty pounds, and he dropped it.

"*Strike two!*" he heard the umpire yell.

"But, but ... " Ward heard himself say.

"You swung, kid. Wait till you see the homework assignment I give you tomorrow." The crowd started throwing things at the umpire. "Boo, hiss," they yelled in protest.

The crowd settled down, a soft breeze started to blow, lightning flashed, and then there was the sound of thunder. A piece of paper blew across left field as someone's radio somewhere far off played "Take Me Out to the Ball Game." Ward dug his back foot into the dirt and looked at the pitcher, who was nodding to the catcher in agreement over the call. Somewhere off right field, a dog barked. The crowd was quiet. The umpire shifted his weight from left to right, and tension started to grow.

The pitcher squinted, slowly looked left, slowly looked right and back to the batter, then wound up for the pitch. All eyes were on Ward as he readied himself. The pitcher's arm flew forward and released the ball. Ward concentrated on that oncoming ball. It was so fast that it caught fire from the friction in the air. Another lightning flash and roll of thunder.

Ward squinted, dug his foot a little deeper, and started his forward swing. The ball reached home plate, where his bat connected with a sharp crack of the ball hitting the metal bat. There was a shower of fireworks and sparks. The ball screamed in pain from the impact. It was heading up, up, up, and the crowd was on its feet, jumping up and down, cheering Ward's name, screaming louder and louder, "Wake up, Ward! Wake up!"

He waved to the crowd as he ran the bases. As he rounded second base, Amanda blew him a kiss and called out, "Wake up, Ward! Wake up!"

As he rounded third base, he took his hat off and waved to the crowd. He saw Mom, Dad, and Little Bit in the bleachers waving and cheering. And he heard his dad saying, "That's my boy!" And he heard his mom yelling, "Wake up, Ward, for the last time!"

Wait? Wake up? Ward sat straight up in his bed and found his mom standing next to him with a cup of water. "One more minute, and this was going to be all over you. Now get up, and get ready for the game, for Pete's sake.

She left the room, and Ward got up and shook his head, whispering, "What a dream."

Ward put on his baseball uniform and went downstairs for breakfast. As he passed the living room, there was Little Bit watching an old Three Stooges movie. The scene was all three of them sitting around a breakfast table. Ward just looked down and shook his head.

"How many pancakes do you want, sport?" he heard a voice say. Quickly he looked up and saw his dad behind the stove.

"That was just too weird," he said in a low voice.

"What's that, Ward?" his dad asked, a little confused.

"Just a really strange dream I had last night, that's all, Dad. May I have five?"

"Five it is," his dad said with a smile.

After breakfast, the four of them walked out the back door to the sidewalk with Little Bit in her stroller. When Ward looked down and hopped over the cracks, his mom said, "Step on a crack, you break your mother's back."

Ward stopped and looked up at her. "What was that?"

"Don't worry. It's just something my mom use to say to me. What's wrong?"

After a moment of quiet, his dad said, "What *is* the matter, Ward? Nervous about the game?"

"Umm, yeah, that must be it," Ward said, a little dazed. "Sorry, I was just thinking that I heard that somewhere else before ..." he answered, his voice trailing off into another thought.

They walked down the sidewalk with the sun directly overhead. It was a beautiful day, not too warm, not too cold, and for the most part, no clouds, except a few dark ones on the horizon.

As they waited in line to get in at the ball field, Ward saw someone on a ladder, hanging a banner over the entry: "Special Guest at Today's Game." His dad said, "Special guest. I wonder who it is."

Ward looked up ahead and saw someone passing out something to the people in line. They were next in line when he could see what it was. They were baseball bats, only these were the blow-up kind. Then he saw a sign next to the entry: "'Free to the first fifty people." As they entered, the guy who was handing out the bats looked at Ward and said, "Are you playing ball with one of the teams today?"

Ward looked down at his uniform, then back at him, kind of sideways, and said, "Yes?"

The man took a step back to the table behind him, grabbed something, and turned back to Ward. "Someone left this here. Would you mind taking it back to the field?"

It was a metal bat. "Stranger and stranger," Ward said under his breath.

"I'm sorry, what was that?" the man asked.

"I mean, yes, sir, I can do that for you," Ward said.

The family walked into the park, and he noticed dark clouds over the ball field with only the sound of thunder. The umpires and coaches were standing at the pitcher's mound, looking up at the clouds, trying to decide if they should let the game go on or not.

When Ward's family got to the edge of the field, his dad stopped him by putting his arm up in front of his bat. He looked down and said, "We are here for you, Ward, your mom and me. We always have been—"

"And always will be," Ward finished in a low voice, looking up at him, feeling as if he were in a dream.

"How did you know I was going to say that?" his father asked, surprised.

"Dad, I had this really crazy dream last night and I—"

"Play ball!" one of the umpires yelled.

On the other side of the field, Mike and Janet had just sat down with their moms. Mike's dad said, "I have to run up to the announcer's box for a minute. Do you want to come with me?" Both Mike and Janet very enthusiastically yelled at the same time, "*Yes*, I want to come." Mike's dad said, "Well, come on then."

They got up to the announcer's box, and Mike's dad said, "I will only be a minute. Look around, but don't touch."

Mike and Janet walked over to the main desk with the microphones. They looked at each other and smiled. Mike pretended he was the announcer and said into the microphone, "Won't you welcome our own local hero ..." That's when *everyone* noticed that the microphone was on. Mike's dad turned around quickly, ran over to them, and shut off the microphone. But it was too late; the crowd thought the game was about to start, so they began to cheer.

Back on the field, Ward looked up and saw Mike and Janet waving at him from the announcer's box. The real announcer then came to the microphone and said, "Welcome to Hamilton's Field on this fine, partly cloudy day. As we advertised, today we have a few special guests."

Ward's coach ran up to him and said, "We need someone to stand on home plate for the special guest. Since you already have a bat, would you please go over and do as they ask?" Without even waiting for an answer, the coach said, "Thanks a lot, Ward. Have fun." The coach ran away, waving at one of the umpires.

Ward looked around the field nervously. His dad, who was still standing beside him with his arm up, said, "What are you looking for, Ward?"

"The black cat," Ward said, kind of confused.

"Black cat? What are you—"

"And now a big round of applause for our special guests," the announcer called, "and the pregame show, the very funny Three Stooges!"

Three guys came out from behind a curtain and ran out onto the field dressed like the Three Stooges, slapping, poking, falling, and jumping for their act. Ward could hardly believe his eyes. After their act, Curly ran over to Ward, who had been waiting on home plate, and he said in a New York accent, "Okay, buddy, here's what we are going to do. You are going to swing three or four times and then run the bases. Budda boom, budda bing, we're done, okay?" Without waiting for an answer, he said, "Great, here we go."

Curly walked over to home plate and circled his hand in the air to signal that it was time to start the show. Moe stepped up to the pitcher's mound, and Larry ran to first base. Ward looked around for Mr. Lees, but did not see him. So he just shrugged his shoulders and watched Moe for the ball. Then he heard behind him, "Hey, kid, hit a homey, nuck, nuck, nuck." But this time it was a lot louder. Then he noticed all three were wearing wireless microphones.

After a little dance at the mound, Moe wound up big for his first pitch. Everyone was cheering and singing when Moe let go of the ball, and to Ward's amazement, it rolled across the turf and then finally across home plate.

"*Strike one!*" yelled the umpire. Ward quickly turned around to see Mr. Lees as the umpire. The crowd started yelling and booing. Ward froze; he didn't know what to do. Then Curly covered his microphone and said, "Just go with it, kid."

Ward snapped out of his fright and yelled, "*What?!*" The crowd went wild with laughter. Mr. Lees lifted his face mask, and before he could say anything, Ward said, "I did turn in my homework."

Mr. Lees said, a little confused, "Um, okay. I wasn't going to say anything about homework, but if you say you did, I believe you."

Moe looked to Curly for the signal. Just then, a fly was buzzing around Curly's face, and he was swatting at it, but Moe thought it was the signal and threw the ball straight up in the air. It sounded like the whole crowd inhaled at the same time just like the dream. "Why, you numbskull, what kind of signal was that?" Moe said into the microphone.

"Aww, buzz off," Curly replied.

"Why I oughta ..." Moe said again, with his voice echoing in the park. The ball landed in front of home plate and rolled across, which made Ward step back. "*Strike two!*"

"*You have to be kidding, right?*" Ward yelled. Again boos erupted from the crowd. Ward smiled from ear to ear.

Mr. Lees looked at the crowd and then put his hands up to quiet them. "Okay, okay. Ball one." The crowd burst out in cheers.

Moe wound up and threw the next pitch, which was way outside. Cameras in the crowd were flashing. Ward moved the bat just a little, and he heard "*Strike two*" from the umpire.

"But, but ... " Ward heard himself say.

"You swung, kid." The crowd started booing and hissing in protest.

The crowd settled down, a soft breeze started to blow, and thunder boomed in the distance. Ward was ready for this; he knew what was going to happen next. He heard over the PA at low volume, "Take me out to the ball game."

From behind him, he heard Curly say in low voice, "Just swing, and let him call you out, kid, so we can get the real game going."

Ward dug his back foot into the dirt and looked at the pitcher, who was nodding to the catcher in agreement of the call. Somewhere off right field, a dog barked. The crowd was quiet, the umpire shifted his weight from left to right, and tension grew.

The pitcher squinted, slowly looked left, slowly looked right and then back to the batter. He wound up for the pitch. All eyes were on Ward as he readied himself. The pitcher's arm flew forward and released the ball. Ward concentrated on the oncoming ball. It was fast, and Ward imagined it catching fire from the friction in the air. Another roll of thunder.

Ward squinted, dug his foot a little deeper, and started his forward swing. The ball reached home plate, where Ward's bat connected with a sharp crack of the ball hitting the metal bat. But there was no shower of fireworks and sparks. Ward was surprised that he'd connected with the ball. It headed up, up, up, and the crowd was standing on their feet, jumping up and down, cheering and screaming louder and louder.

"Go on, run the bases, kid," Curly yelled. Everyone watched the ball fly into center field, where it was chased by none other than Wayne, a.k.a. the Night Crawler. Ward didn't notice him at first, so he started running the bases and waving to the crowd. As he rounded second base, he looked for Amanda. She wasn't on the field, but he saw her in the stands, waving. He tipped his hat to her like one of the pro baseball players.

As he rounded third base, he took his hat off and waved to the crowd. He saw Mom, Dad, and Little Bit in the bleachers, waving and cheering. And he heard his dad say, "That's my boy!" He could hear his mom yelling, "Look behind you!"

Ward thought, *That's not what she should be saying.* Then he realized this was real and not some dream. He turned to see the Night Crawler running after him with the ball, yelling, "You're mine, dirtbag."

Ward was so shaken, he ran faster, zigzagging between third and home; he ran straight for Moe at the pitcher's mound. The crowd thought it was part of the show, so they laughed and cheered for Ward.

The two ran around Moe twice, and on the third time, Moe stuck out his foot and tripped Wayne. The crowd cheered even louder. Ward ran straight for home plate, but Wayne was quick to get back on his feet and again was running after him.

The crowd was standing and cheering for Ward to make it to home plate; the noise was almost deafening. He was almost there, with Wayne right behind him. Wayne's arm was fully extended, and he was leaning forward, trying to touch Ward. At the last second, Ward leaned forward himself and touched home plate. Then Wayne touched him.

It was a photo finish, and the crowd went wild with cheers and laughter. Curly grabbed Ward as he was picking up his bat to help get him away from Wayne, and the umpire stuck out his foot and tripped Wayne again. He fell flat.

Moe looked to the crowd for a ruling on the play. Over the PA, he said, "Okay, boys and girls. Cheer if you think our batter did not make it." About a dozen people cheered.

"Okay, cheer if you think our batter did make it." The whole stadium broke out in a very loud cheer, with people jumping up and down, clapping and whistling.

"Unbelievable," Moe said into the microphone.

Wayne got to his feet and tried one more time to get Ward, but Moe saw this coming and got Curly to help put Ward on their shoulders to parade around, while Ward waved with one hand and waved the bat with the other. Larry got in between the two boys so Wayne could not get ahold of Ward.

The Three Stooges ended their pregame show by carrying Ward off the field. As soon as they were off the field, the announcer for the game came back on and said, "Was that some show or what? Let's give one more round of applause for the *Three Stooges*, ladies and gentlemen." The crowd cheered louder.

As the announcer made some announcements about upcoming events, behind the bleachers the Three Stooges put Ward back down on the ground. Moe looked around for Wayne and asked, "Who was that kid? I thought he was going to ruin things. Are you going to be okay, sport?"

"I'll be fine. He goes to my school and takes our lunch money every day. We call him the Night

Crawler because when he was a baby he used to get out of his crib at night. He probably still does. I don't know."

The three guys started to laugh. Then Larry said, "Hey, kid, I think you have an admirer over there." He pointed over his shoulder.

Ward turned around and saw Amanda looking as beautiful as ever. He said, "Come here, Amanda, I want to introduce you to my new friends."

As she walked over, the three did the famous "Hello," "Hello," "Hellooooo," and then in unison "Hello." Amanda blushed a little and then shook their hands.

A photographer came over and said, "Hi, I'm with the *Daily Times,* and I would like to get a picture of you guys."

Ward said, "Come on, Amanda, let's get out of the way."

The photograph said, "No, no, no, I need you in the picture too. And if your girlfriend wants, she can be in it also."

Ward stammered, "I … umm … she … "

"That's okay. I don't mind," Amanda said, looking at Ward.

"Well, okay then," Ward said. "Shoot away."

They stood in front of the Three Stooges, and the three did different things behind them. After about a dozen or so shots, the photographer said, "Thanks a lot. I think I have what I need," and he walked away. The Three Stooges said their good-byes to the two kids and walked off too, poking, pushing, and laughing as they walked away to their car.

Mike and Janet came running up, and the four of them stood there for about ten minutes, talking about the pregame show and how fun and funny it was. The three told Ward what a great job he'd done and asked if they'd practiced the show before they went out. "Practiced?" Ward said. "Well, kind of."

Just then a voice behind Ward said, "Okay, butthead, now you're mine."

Ward turned around so fast, he forgot he still had the bat in his hand. He hit Wayne right in the groin, which made him go straight to the ground. But that's not all. As Wayne was falling to the ground, Ward hadn't moved the bat, and Wayne hit his forehead on it on the way down—a two-for-one hit.

Wayne was switching from rubbing his head to his groin when *he* heard a familiar voice: "What are you doing on the ground? Get up and dust yourself off, boy." It was Wayne's dad. Wayne got up quickly, and his dad said, "Are you picking on these kids? I warned you about that, didn't I?"

"Oh, no, sir." Ward said. "We were just talking about ... about the ... about the game, sir. Night ... I mean, Wayne just tripped. Is he okay?" The other three looked at him, very, *very* surprised.

Wayne's dad said, "Oh, I'm sorry. I thought he was picking on you and your friends. I warned him that someday it would come back on him." Then he turned to Wayne and said a little more sympathetically, "I'm sorry, son, are you okay? Let's go home. Your mom cooked a real nice lunch." As they started to walk away, Wayne turned around and looked back at Ward and his friends for a moment. Then he smiled.

When they were far enough away, Mike grabbed Ward by the shirt, shook him back and forth, and said in a harsh whisper, "Are you crazy?! Do you know what he is going to do to you on Monday?"

Ward just smiled and said, "No, I think things are going to be different from now on." With a smile, he looked at Amanda and said, "Yep, different from now on."

For the rest of the day, Ward could not stop smiling. As he played with Little Bit, he seemed more relaxed and worry-free. After dinner, he cleared the table as he whistled "Take Me Out to the Ball Game." When he was done, he took Little Bit up to her room to get ready for bed.

His mom went into the living room, where his dad was sitting on the couch, watching the news. She sat down beside him and said, "I wonder what got into him?" Just then the news anchor started to talk about the pregame show with the Three Stooges and how they'd raised $650 for a local charity. Near the end of the report was a shot of four kids laughing and joking behind the reporter.

"I don't believe it," Ward's mom said. "He got on TV with his friends! Aww, and we didn't tape it."

"I don't think he is going to need a video of this day to help him remember it. He's got his friend to relive it anytime he wants. And having friends is better than any videotape."